An Accomplished Lady (of the Best Sort)

A TEATIME TALES NOVELETTE

LEENIE BROWN

Leenie B Books
Halifax

ISBNs: (ebook) 978-1-990607-25-7; (paperback) 978-1-990607-26-4; (large print) 978-1-990607-27-1

www.leeniebbooks.com

www.leeniebrown.com

Chapter 1

THE DOOR TO THE library closed, and Charles Bingley listened carefully to the sound of footsteps growing faint as distance separated his sisters from him. When he could not hear even the softest step, he turned to his friend.

"Come, Darcy, tell us what troubles you," he said as he fiddled with the deck of cards that had been left on the table when his sisters had left the room. He hoped that in doing so it would look like he was just beginning a conversation of little weight.

His dearest friend, Fitzwilliam Darcy, shook his head.

"They will not be returning if that is what has you troubled," Bingley's brother-in-law Hurst inserted. "When Louisa and Caroline begin whispering as they were at the end of our game and paying not one whit of attention to their cards, I know they will be secreted away somewhere for hours."

Darcy gave him a tight smile. "It is nothing of significance."

Bingley placed the deck of cards back on the table and tapped the top of them before rising from his chair. "Then, it should cause you little pain to share your thoughts." He paced to the hearth and gave what remained of the fire a stir. The nights were definitely growing colder, but this room seemed well-suited to keeping out drafts – or most of them – as long as the door was closed.

He turned toward his resolutely silent friend and shot Hurst a conspiratorial smile. "I dare say he either has no thoughts, or he thinks us too stupid to hear them."

"I do not –" Darcy began, but then stopped and said, "No, you will not draw it out of me by tricks."

"Would libations work?" Hurst asked.

Darcy chuckled. "No. I prefer to keep my own counsel is all."

"Well, that is too bad. I was hoping for a glass of something that would burn my throat a bit."

"Do not let me stop you," Darcy replied. "If your brother has something of the sort to offer, let him offer it."

"He knows where he can find it." Bingley dropped down on a sofa across from Darcy. "He just wants an excuse to indulge more than my sister would find appropriate for one of his station."

"I am not hen-pecked, if that is what you are implying."
Bingley shrugged.

He knew just how demanding his older sister could be. If her husband were not at least a little hen-pecked, it would be a miracle – or he would be some grizzled old military man, who was slightly hard of hearing and who barked orders at one and all without ever taking one himself. That was not Hurst. Hurst tended towards self-indulgence in most things, but most significantly, fashion, cards, and drinking. He was not a drunkard, but then, that might be partly due to Louisa's constant nattering on the subject.

"I suppose then, Hurst, that we shall have to guess the source of the frown that has furrowed the place between Darcy's eyes."

"I am not frowning. I am thinking."

"It does rather look the same," Hurst inserted.

"Do you think he is considering our sister as a wife?" Bingley knew the answer to that question, which was precisely the reason why he had posed it.

Darcy groaned and shook his head. "I said that I would not succumb to trickery, and I am a man of my word."

"I am not attempting to trick you. I am attempting to formulate a reason for your sullen behaviour so that you will not have to tell us." Bingley extended his legs and crossed his ankles. "I am providing a service. Now, if you would kindly refrain from interrupting my process."

"Your process?" Darcy cried. "I know your process. You shall concoct the most ridiculous reason designed in every detail to provoke me into proving you wrong. It is what you always do."

"If you know you are going to have to tell him, I do not see why you allow yourself the misery of bearing his schemes," Hurst said. "It seems rather a good deal better to just offer the information at the first."

"Can I not just ponder things on my own without sharing them with you two housewives?"

"You can if you will do so quietly while I concoct a most ridiculous reason," Bingley replied with a smile.

"Why do I tolerate you?" Darcy growled.

"Because I am amiable and easily led."

Darcy chuckled. "Easily led? You? Do you believe that, Hurst?"

"There is not a Bingley of my acquaintance of either sex who does not do precisely as he or she wishes to do."

"He is rather obstinate, is he not?" Darcy gave Bingley a taunting smile.

"Well, then, I do believe it is merely my charm which endears me to you." Bingley sat forward, clasped his hands under his chin, and fluttered his lashes.

"Do not do that," Hurst said on the end of a laugh. "Expressions such as that can put a man off his food and keep him from sleeping at night."

"In that case, I shall teach it to your son when you have one."

"You will do nothing of the sort," Hurst retorted.

"There is no news on that front is there?" Bingley knew that his sister had been hopeful twice in the past year and a half that she might be with child, only to be disappointed.

"None that has been told to me."

"My condolences," Darcy said.

"Thank you." Hurst shrugged and fell silent.

Oh, well, that was well done! How was he supposed to entertain himself and discover if Darcy's thoughts regarding Miss Elizabeth Bennet were favourable or not if both his companions refused to carry a conversation?

"I do hope Miss Bennet is better in the morning," he said in an attempt to start some sort of discussion.

This was met with two muttered agreements and nothing else.

"I think I might wish to marry her." There. That should get some sort of response beyond a mutter.

"Louisa and Caroline have already supposed that was the direction in which you had set your mind."

"Have they?" Darcy's tone was as surprised sounding as Bingley felt at Hurst's revelation.

"Why do you think they disparage the Bennets so much?"

"I thought it was because Darcy finds Miss Elizabeth fascinating," Bingley answered.

Hurst shrugged. "There is that. However, your interest in the eldest Miss Bennet would bring the whole family into our circle of close friends and relations, which happens to include Darcy. And you know Caroline does not like to lose or even think she might."

Well, that was true. Caroline was spoiled and crafty. Bingley could think of several times in their younger years when she had arranged to win at some game by bribing a servant or enacting some scheme to cripple her opponent's chances. He sat forward as a thought struck him.

"Are they devising a scheme to ensure that Darcy is not given more time to become attached to Miss Elizabeth?"

Hurst shook his head. "I am sure I could not say, but I would be on my guard if I were you."

"Darcy is not going to become more attached to Miss Elizabeth," Darcy answered. "Darcy is not attached to Miss Elizabeth. She is an acquaintance and a momentary diversion. Nothing else."

Bingley chuckled. "And yet, you have been sitting there pondering what she said about accomplished ladies for over an hour."

Darcy blinked. "How did –" He pressed his lips together and shook his head. "No, no, I shall not engage your guess."

"Then, I am correct in my assessment?"

"I dare say you are," Hurst agreed. "His ears are turning red."

Darcy rose. "I honestly do not see why I tolerate the two of you."

"Sit down."

"I am going to my room."

"Then, expect me to question you about this tomorrow." Bingley crossed his arms and glared at Darcy. The man was as stubborn as a mule at times. "You do know that we are capable of helping you figure out whatever it is that you are pondering. In fact, I know from experience that you often come to a conclusion much more readily when you begin to reason aloud."

"But reasoning aloud means others will hear my thoughts."

"He is brilliant, is he not, Hurst?"

Hurst held up his hands. "I rather like my face as it is. I shall let you decide this between yourselves alone."

"You are such a coward," Bingley shot back at him.

"Perhaps, but I am a handsome one, and I intend to keep it that way."

"Debating my thoughts with you will do me no good, for I already know your opinion on the matter."

"Do you?" Bingley said along with Hurst.

"I believe your words were that you would not be as fastidious as me for a kingdom or something rather close to that. Therefore, I already know that you think my standards for what I consider a properly accomplished lady are too exacting. You know, for instance, that I would not approve of Miss Bennet for you if you were to petition me for my opinion on the matter because her circumstances are not as high as I would recommend. They are not overly low, but they are not as elevated as many of the ladies you have called on in town."

Bingley's mouth dropped open. This was what his friend thought of the angel who rested in one of the guest chambers above stairs? She was not good enough for him? Him, who was not yet a landed gentleman? Him who thought his heart likely already lost to the sweetest lady he had ever been fortunate enough to meet? Of all the ridiculous thoughts to have had, that had to be the most incredulously absurd one that Bingley had ever heard Darcy spout.

"And now I have offended you, which is precisely why I should not have aired even one of my thoughts."

Bingley rose from the sofa and came to stand in front of his dearest and currently stupidest friend. He'd be hanged if he was going to let the fellow get away with disparaging Miss Bennet. "I was wrong. You are not merely fastidious. You are arrogant and priggish. I dare say you tolerate me because you know that if you do not, you will be left without a particular friend because I am the only one who can put up with your high in the instep attitude without demanding you relieve me of my duty to my youngest sister in return for the favour."

Darcy's eyes had narrowed as Bingley spoke. It was obvious that the man was more than a little angry, but to Bingley's way of thinking, it was precisely what he deserved.

"I see I have offend the great and mighty Fitzwilliam Darcy. I suppose he was correct about it being better to keep one's thoughts in one's head." He turned to Hurst. "I think you and I should provoke my sister and have a glass of something rather strong. What say you?" He moved a pace away from Darcy. "I hope you sleep as you deserve. Good night, sir." He made a motion towards the door.

"May your wish be granted to you in kind," Darcy said before stalking out of the room.

"That was not well-done," Hurst said when the door had closed behind Darcy. "If we lose his connection, it will hurt Caroline's chances of making a good match."

"If we keep his connection, she will never consider anyone other than him as a match." Bingley's cheeks puffed out before he blew out a breath. Darcy was angry, but he doubted that what had been said would end their friendship. They had spoken harshly to one another before and, after a period of time, things had been restored. He ran a hand through his hair. He certainly hoped that this would be one of those times and not some new thing.

"What I said needed to be said." He rubbed his chin. He was nearly certain he was right about that. "If I had not said what I did now, eventually, he would meet with someone who might."

Hurst chuckled. "I do think your Miss Bennet's next youngest sister might have stepped up to complete the task if given the opportunity. She does tend to provoke him, and he, her in return."

"Do you think he is wrong about his qualifications for an accomplished lady?" Bingley's sister Caroline had given quite the demanding list of criteria for being considered an accomplished lady, and then Darcy had added to it – as if Caroline's list was short a few!

"I think he might hold to them too tightly."

Bingley paced a circle around the sofa. "And if he were to choose a wife on those qualifications…" He shook his head. It would not be the one lady who had ever seemed to capture Darcy's attention.

"The poor man would be miserable," Hurst concluded.

A smile tipped one side of Bingley's mouth as he stopped pacing. "Then, perhaps, my dear brother, we should take it upon ourselves to show him his error."

Hurst's eyes grew wide. "How... how do you propose we do that?"

"I am not precisely sure, but I am certain we can do it."

"Louisa is not going to like this, is she?"

Bingley laughed as he opened a decanter of port. "No. Not even a little bit."

Chapter 2

BINGLEY TURNED AWAY FROM his careful study of Miss Bennet's door as he heard footsteps coming towards him. Darcy did not look pleased about something. But then, he really had not looked pleased about much of anything since he had arrived in Hertfordshire.

"Why are the youngest Miss Bennets in the drawing room?" his friend demanded softly as he came to stand next to him.

Ah, yes, the local riffraff. Their presence in Darcy's precious world of propriety-at-all costs would annoy him. Bingley shrugged. "I suppose it is because they wished to see the place. At least, that is what I gleaned from the exclamations of proper delight from Miss Lydia upon entering."

And truly there was no other reason for them to have accompanied their mother. It was not as if either Miss Lydia or Miss Kitty could do anything to help their eldest sister. Indeed, according to their mother, they were not wanted in the sick room.

"Did they arrive upon your doorstep requesting a tour? That seems rather forward of them, and I will mark it in your mind that such behaviour does not recommend their family as one to which to tie oneself."

Bingley sighed. He was in no frame of mind to put up with a Darcy who had not yet fully forgiven him for his speech last night and who was looking for instances in which to prove himself correct.

"No, we would not wish to be associated with any more disagreeable relations than those with whom we are already burdened through certain connections." He gave Darcy a pointed look. "Do not tell me that you have forgotten your aunt's inquisition of me upon our first meeting? I fully expected her to lift my foot to inspect the soles of my boots before taking a look at my teeth. I am surprised her favourite nephew did not take her advice to disassociate himself from one who was so closely tied to trade."

"Her nephew may still do so," Darcy grumbled.

"Do as you see fit." Bingley turned back to what he had been doing – waiting impatiently for Mr. Jones to reappear from Miss Bennet's room to tell him how she fared.

"Why are the youngest Miss Bennets here?" Darcy asked.

"Because their mother was summoned to evaluate her daughter's condition, and they came with her."

At this, Darcy looked genuinely concerned. "Has Miss Bennet grown worse?"

"According to her sister both last night after you left Hurst and me and again this morning when I inquired through a maid, yes. That is why Mr. Jones arrived a few minutes ago. I am just waiting to hear if any further assistance is needed."

"Would you send to town for your doctor?"

"If needed."

"I could send for mine."

Bingley arched a brow as he glanced at his friend. "Feeling charitable to those beneath your notice, are you?"

Darcy was not the only one who had not fully recovered from last night's argument. It still rankled in a way nothing ever had rankled Bingley before that his friend did not approve of the lady who had captured his attention.

"Beneath my what?" Darcy sputtered. "About what are you speaking?"

Bingley gave his friend a perplexed look. Was the man really so dense? "I believe that both yesterday and just now you have cautioned me that Miss Bennet is not good enough for me," he whispered.

"I did not say she was not good enough. I said the match would not be advantageous," Darcy protested.

"I do not see the difference in the two statements, nor do I wish to give the topic any further consideration. Leave me to my ignorance and my guest. I will do my best to be understanding if you refuse to keep my acquaintance after I marry."

"Why –" Darcy looked from Bingley to the door to Miss Bennet's room and back. "Have you decided to marry her?"

"Nearly." Bingley scrubbed his face. "I have been awake half the night worrying about if she is well or not. Do you think you could hold your lecture about deciding such things too quickly or how marrying for love might not be prudent until later?"

"Marrying for love? Imprudent?" Darcy shook his head. "You truly think that I would wish for you to marry without love?"

"Only if the lady's family was unacceptable, it seems. Now, please, go away."

A pained expression settled on Darcy's features. Apparently, he was beginning to see something other than his own offense. "Do you want me to leave Netherfield?"

Or more precisely, Bingley amended his thought, Darcy had just cottoned on to how offensive he had been and was likely already chastising himself for it far more than he should. The man truly was the reigning monarch of jumping from one extreme to another in a heartbeat.

Bingley shook his head. "I just want to fret over the wellbeing of the lovely lady in that room without having to defend myself to you for doing so. Please, just leave me be."

Darcy held Bingley's gaze for half a minute before giving a firm shake of his head and saying, "No."

"What do you mean, *no*?"

Darcy's lips tipped into a small grin. "Tell me about her. What, besides her beauty, makes you think you are in love with her?"

"Now?"

Darcy nodded.

"Here? In the corridor?"

Again, Darcy nodded. "Unless you would like to find a room where we can have this discussion. I am certain a maid or footman can see to it that Mr. Jones finds us before he leaves." He blew out a breath and began to look excessively uneasy. "Perhaps I have been too hasty in my judgment about Miss Bennet."

An apology? So quickly? Well, this was a surprising, though not unwelcome, turn of events! However, before Bingley could do more than weigh the options of where to have their discussion, the door in front of them opened.

"How is she?" Bingley pushed off the wall against which he had been leaning and met Mr. Jones in the middle of the hallway.

"I would not subject her to being moved, but she is not in grave danger as long as she rests as she has been and follows my instructions." The apothecary straightened his jacket with the hand which was not holding his bag of remedies. "I believe Miss Elizabeth has them all written down and will not deviate from the plan. If she were not a gentlewoman, she would make a fine assistant to my apprentice." He glanced back at the door to Miss Bennet's room.

"You have an apprentice?" Darcy asked with curiosity.

Mr. Jones chuckled. "My son. Miss Elizabeth will make some gentleman a fine wife some day if he is not too ignorant to appreciate a keen mind. I was just once again wishing it would be my son." He chuckled again. "But it will not be. If I am not needed for anything else, I will be off."

"There is no need for concern, then?" Bingley needed to be certain that all was well.

"None above seeing that proper care is given and sending for me if the prescribed treatment does not do what it is intended to do."

"And will that take long? How often should I check?"

Mr. Jones chuckled again. "You are most solicitous. But then, Miss Bennet is rather beautiful, is she not?"

Bingley felt his cheeks warm at the implication of the man's words, but he could not refute them. "She is, and I will not deny that such a fact might make me more prone to be prompt in my solicitude, but I would like to think I would be just as concerned for another, less attractive and sweet guest in my home."

"I have no doubt that you would be. I have heard nothing but good things about you, Mr. Bingley. Fortune has shined on us in adding you to our community, but I did want to discover for myself if the rumours of a possible attachment were founded on more than a mother's hope."

"Are there rumours?" Darcy asked in surprise.

Again, Bingley gave his friend a baffled look. Where had the man been for the past month? How could he not know that there were rumours?

"I danced with her twice, Darcy. I believe even you commented on that fact." And in doing so had instructed him that raising hopes in such a way was not the thing to do – especially on such short acquaintance and in a new area where the families were not known to him.

"Right." Darcy looked somewhat chagrined. "It seems that fact slipped my mind for a moment."

"My friend is not one to gossip or engage in speculation too often," Bingley explained to Mr. Jones.

"I have heard that Mr. Darcy seems to know his mind and keep his own counsel and only shares it with those who are of his party."

"Have I offended someone?" Darcy asked Mr. Jones as he and Bingley began walking toward the staircase with the man.

Mr. Jones tipped his head in the direction from which they had just come.

"Mrs. Bennet?"

Mr. Jones gave one nod of his head. "She may not always approve of Miss Elizabeth's fondness for knowledge, but no one, no matter their rank, will be looked on fondly if that person declares her daughters to be lacking in any way. To be honest, I cannot blame her for it."

Darcy's lips twitched into a quick and tight smile. "A word spoken in haste and to quell great provocation is never good and often far from the truth."

That brought a chuckle from the apothecary. "You did not strike me as ignorant. I am glad to know my assessment was correct. Now, I will take my leave of you. Please send word if I am needed."

"I will," Bingley assured him.

"I am just as you said last night." Darcy rubbed the back of his neck. "I am arrogant and priggish and apparently not well-liked in the community or even in your home. Of course, until this moment, I have not cared what the community thought of me, but..." His cheeks puffed out as he blew out a breath.

"Do you still wish to hear about Miss Bennet?" Bingley asked cautiously.

"It seems I need to, and perhaps, we should not stop there. I may need to hear how you view all of the area, for I may have been at fault about it all."

Yes, the man did jump from one side of a chasm to another as easily as others put one foot in front of another, but at least, having him on the side of the divide that put him in a more favourable place to discover his fascination with Miss Elizabeth might be more than a momentary diversion was not a bad thing in Bingley's mind.

Chapter 3

"HE APOLOGIZED," BINGLEY WHISPERED to Hurst as he entered the drawing room where the youngest Bennets were providing his sisters with copious amounts of material about which he was certain they would laugh later.

"Indeed?" Hurst said in surprise. "So soon?"

"Yes, and I do believe we are well positioned to proceed as planned." He turned to Miss Lydia and Miss Kitty. "I am pleased to report that your sister is expected to make a full recovery in due time."

"That is excellent news." Caroline's eyes followed Darcy as he took a seat as far away from her as he could. "Do you not agree, Mr. Darcy? Is it not the most fortunate news we could have?"

Darcy shifted uneasily in his chair. "Happy news about a sister is always welcome."

"Have you had a letter from your sister? Is she doing well?" Louisa inserted.

"You have a sister?" Miss Lydia asked. "Why is she not with you? I would be very sorry indeed to be left behind by my brother if he were travelling to a place as lovely as Netherfield." She tipped her head and her brow furrowed.

"That is if I had a brother," she added. "I think it would be lovely to have a brother, do you not agree, Kitty?"

"Oh, I could not agree more."

Upon this assurance they were both in agreement, the youngest Bennets fell silent and looked expectantly at Darcy, whose expression held a bit of amusement to it. That was a good sign as far as Bingley was concerned for it meant his friend was predisposed to enter the conversation with interest rather than with merely a critical eye.

"As a matter of fact, I do have a sister, and if I am allowed to be so bold as to guess without being thought altogether too forward, I would imagine that you, Miss Lydia, are about her age."

"Is she fifteen?"

Miss Lydia did not look offended by Darcy's guess at all. Her eyes were as round as the saucers under the cups on a tea tray, and her lashes only fluttered twice. That seemed impressive to Bingley, who had noted just how frequently that particular Bennet fluttered her lashes. He wondered if Darcy had observed that or if he had been too focused on the overall behaviour of the Bennets being unacceptable to notice such details.

"I am fifteen," Miss Lydia continued, "and Kitty just turned seventeen."

"Georgiana is sixteen, and she also just had a birthday."

Darcy was still looking somewhat amused, and a trifle relaxed, compared to how Bingley had often seen him in company with people he did not know very well. That was also a good sign. Perhaps their short talk about what Bingley found to love about Miss Bennet, besides her beauty, had begun to soften the man.

"Georgiana." The name was more of a sigh than spoken by Miss Kitty. "That is such a pretty name."

"Allow me to thank you on my sister's behalf. It was my grandmother's name."

This also elicited a sigh from Miss Kitty. If Bingley were to place a wager on which of the youngest Bennets was the most given to romantic fancies, he would place every pound he was betting on Miss Kitty.

"Why is your sister not with you?"

"Lydia," Miss Elizabeth scolded as she joined her sisters on the settee and cast a wary eye at Caroline.

Bingley sighed. His sisters were such bothers at times.

"It is not polite to pry into things that do not concern you," Miss Elizabeth continued.

Miss Lydia rolled her eyes and huffed. If Bingley had to wager on which of the youngest Bennets who, with a bit of training, could outdo his sisters for cattiness, his money was on Miss Lydia.

"I am not offended by the inquiry," Darcy said. "Georgiana is in town with our aunt so that she can continue her lessons and because she has not been feeling quite herself lately."

Miss Lydia's hand flew to her heart. "That is dreadful! I do hope it is nothing serious that has her feeling unwell."

"Your concern does you credit," Darcy assured her. "She is just a trifle melancholy."

Miss Lydia shook her head and made a small clucking noise. "It really is too bad that she must continue her studies, for if she were not obliged to do so, she could have joined you and then, we could have cheered her up. Is that not right, Kitty?"

"Oh, for certain. We are very good at being cheerful and having fun."

The little bit of sorrow that had clouded Darcy's expression as he had spoken of his sister was replaced by a smile that was neither forced nor condescending but was rather a completely natural expression.

Hurst coughed, catching Bingley's attention, and then, he raised his eyebrows in question. Bingley simply shrugged. It seemed that his friend was capable of not only jumping from recognition of error to utter despondence over it but also possessed the ability to affect a transformation of his position on a subject in very short order.

"What is your favourite amusement?" Bingley asked the youngest Bennets as Mrs. Bennet finally joined them.

"Dancing," Miss Lydia answered.

That did not surprise Bingley.

"Drawing," Miss Kitty replied.

That did surprise him. He had expected that Miss Kitty would like whatever it was that Miss Lydia did.

"Kitty is the best at drawing of all my sisters," Miss Lydia said. "And I am the best at dancing."

"So, all of your sisters draw?" Mr. Hurst asked.

"Oh, yes, Father insisted that we at least attempt it. I fear I am quite dreadful at it, but then, I have Kitty to draw things for me, so it is not so bad, you see."

"My husband has made certain that our daughters have made an attempt at learning many things," Mrs. Bennet inserted.

"Has he indeed?" Darcy was leaned forward in his seat a bit as if he were truly interested.

"Indeed, he has," Mrs. Bennet assured him. "There is more than beauty to be found in my daughters." One eyebrow arched, and she gave him a pointed look. "Even Mary is pretty in her own way. None of them can compare to Jane in that regard or Lydia when it comes to liveliness, but they each have their own particular areas in which they excel."

"I am certain they do."

"What does your sister like to do?" Miss Lydia asked, which was too bad since Bingley had hoped Mrs. Bennet would press her point about Darcy's slight of her second eldest daughter a bit further.

"She favours music," Darcy replied.

"Dancing?" Miss Lydia asked hopefully.

He shook his head. "No, she prefers to play or sing."

"She does not like dancing?" Miss Lydia's tone was one of complete disbelief.

"It is not that she does not like it, it is that she does not prefer it."

Miss Lydia's brow furrowed for a moment, but then smoothed as a smile returned to her lips. "Mary prefers playing to dancing."

"Yes," Mrs. Bennet said, "Mary does like to play."

There was a tightness to the Bennet matriarch's expression, and to Bingley it seemed that her tone as she made her agreement spoke to the fact that she wished Miss Mary did not favour playing. He made a mental note to not request a performance from that particular Bennet.

"Elizabeth would rather sing than play, but she is an excellent dancer, though not as good as me." Miss Lydia seemed determined to carry the conversation. "Which do you prefer?" she asked Caroline.

"I do all three quite well, as a well-trained lady should," Caroline replied with a sidelong glance at Miss Elizabeth.

Bingley's eyes narrowed. The catty thing! Must she always be attempting to lift herself up by trampling on others?

"Do you believe, then, that all properly instructed ladies can sing, dance, and play with excellence? And do you credit it only to their training or is it something more?"

To Bingley's delight, Miss Elizabeth had risen to the subtle challenge Caroline had given her. Now, the discussion should turn lively.

"Even a natural talent can be increased by instruction," Caroline replied.

"I do not disagree, but do you think that a lady with no ear for music and the inability to count a rhythm can be taught in such a way as to make her proficient in every area?"

Mrs. Bennet laughed – a bit uneasily as she cast a glance at Bingley. She had no reason to fear. He was not going to be put off his pursuit of Miss Bennet by a disagreement between his troublesome youngest sister and Miss Elizabeth.

"You do ask the strangest questions, Elizabeth," Mrs. Bennet said with another glance in his direction. "Of course, a goose cannot be made to sing like a lark no matter what time and attention is given to the attempt of making it possible." She then looked around the group as if she expected one and all to be in accord with her thoughts on the matter.

Bingley was, but from the look on his sisters' faces, they were not. Darcy's left eyebrow had arched, and he appeared to be on the verge of speaking his thoughts on the matter, so Bingley kept his approbation to himself. Thankfully, his friend did not disappoint.

"I think what you have said is quite true," Darcy said when all others remained silent. "I, for one, could never quite play the violin as smoothly as my tutor did. It did not matter how long I practised or what reward was promised to me for my success. I simply could not count and play all at the same time. However, my sister seems to possess the ability for the music to rise within her and a flow out as naturally as a river winds its way through the hills and valleys."

Bingley held up a finger. Now was the perfect time to enter the discussion and cause great consternation for his sister. Bless Darcy for giving him the opportunity! "Does that mean then," he said, "that only ladies who possess such a gift can ever be considered accomplished?" From the corner of his eye, he saw Hurst's lips curl into a smile.

"I should hope not!" Mrs. Bennet cried. "For if that is what is needed, then no lady could ever be considered accomplished, for I am certain that there is not one of us who possesses such ability in all the necessary skills to be considered accomplished as some define it."

"How would you describe an accomplished lady?" Bingley asked curiously. "We had a discussion about this yesterday, and I will admit that I have been contemplating it ever since." And he suspected that her idea of accomplishments was not the same as those of his sisters.

Mrs. Bennet sat a little straighter and lifted her chin. "Well, now, let me see. To me, an accomplished lady is one who can manage her household well, see that her family is well-clothed, arrange rooms and décor to a most pleasing effect, discern a good servant from a poor one, retain those who are in her employ because she is not a trial to serve, and can design and present an evening of entertainment for her family and circle of friends and neighbours." She paused for a moment but did not look as if she was finished, so Bingley held his tongue and waited.

"She is also kind and generous to those in her care. She always has time to hear the concerns of her tenants and loves her family as no other ever could." She paused once again, then nodded. "Yes, I do believe that is what I would consider an accomplished lady, and I assure you that my husband and I have done our best to see that our daughters can or will be able to do all those things.

Bingley had to admit that her definition of an accomplished lady had surprised him, for he had not truly expected such a well-thought-out answer from her since, in his short acquaintance with her, she seemed disposed to flit and flutter in her way of speaking. From how silent the room currently was, he was certain that he was not alone in his surprise.

"I did not hear you list dancing or playing or singing or drawing or languages, or any of the regular things that are normally purported as necessary for the title," he commented.

Mrs. Bennet looked at him as if he were a confused young lad. "I assure you that they are there. You just cannot see them since they are the things that help each lady accomplish what is necessarily her responsibility in a family. As Mr. Bennet has often said, 'What good is it, my dear, if our daughters can all paint as well as any master if they cannot tell their maids what needs to be done or provide their cook with what is needed to create a meal?' and I agree with him."

"My mother is very good at what she does," Miss Elizabeth said with a smile for Mrs. Bennet.

It was the first time Bingley had seen such affection being shared between Miss Elizabeth and her mother. It had appeared at all other times as if they were constantly at odds. It was comforting to know that the family ties in the Bennet home, though sometimes strained, were strong.

"But if one is to travel in higher circles, rather than just in the country, one's abilities must be more narrowly defined, and her accomplishments must be more classical and less rustic," Caroline inserted.

"I would suppose that if she had a keen mind, then, such a lady would be able to adapt to whatever circumstances in which she found herself," Hurst said.

"You suppose so, do you?" Louisa asked in surprise.

"I do. A keen mind seems necessary."

"I would agree," Bingley said. "What do you say, Darcy?"

"Yes, Mr. Darcy, what do you say?" There was a note of laughter in Caroline's tone. Did she truly think she understood his mind so well as to assume his answer would suit her own? Bingley shook his head. She was about to be disappointed yet again.

Darcy's brow furrowed, and he scowled just the slightest bit – a tell-tale sign that he was thinking deeply. Then, after a moment, he began his response.

"I say that I have not considered a lady's accomplishments as Mrs. Bennet has stated them, nor have I put any effort into considering Hurst's addition to the conversation. However, I have always known that any lady whom I found truly accomplished would have a quick wit and intelligence equal or superior to my own, and for that reason, I do see the possibility that both Mrs. Bennet and Mr. Hurst are correct."

A frown momentarily settled on Caroline's face before she replaced it with a forced look of delight at his reply. Her posturing was pointless. Darcy was never going to choose Caroline as his wife not matter how much she tried to agree with him even when she did not.

"Are you saying then," Miss Elizabeth asked, with no little amount of incredulity to her tone, "that a lady's greatest accomplishment is having a mind that is eager to learn?"

Darcy sat silently for a moment with his eyes fixed on Miss Elizabeth's face. Slowly, his lips curled into a genuinely happy and relieved expression. "I do believe that that is precisely what I am saying."

Bingley shared a surreptitious look with Hurst. It appeared their plan to prove to Darcy that Miss Elizabeth was an accomplished lady worthy of his consideration had met with success before they had expected it would, and who would have thought that their greatest ally in gaining that success would be Mrs. Bennet?

Chapter 4

"Do you now admit that Miss Elizabeth is an accomplished lady?" Bingley asked when the gentlemen were the only ones who remained in the dinning room after their meal. He had been wishing to ask Darcy that question all day, but with some difficulty, he had refrained so that his contemplative friend would have ample time to ponder the thought.

"In her mother's opinion, perhaps." Darcy swirled his port and did not lift his eyes from watching the motion of the red liquid moving up and down and around the glass.

"Perhaps?" Hurst cried. "I daresay is no *perhaps* about it. Miss Elizabeth is an accomplished lady with a quick intellect. We know that she dances well, and that she is a great reader. We also know that she holds the ability to debate a matter in as logical a way as any with whom we attended school. Added to that, she is caring enough to walk three miles to tend to a sick sister and then, remains at that sister's side despite having to deal with the likes of you and Bingley's sisters."

"The likes of me?" Darcy drew and expelled a great breath. "I have been somewhat of a trial, have I not been?"

"There is no *somewhat* about it," Bingley said with a laugh. "But we are used to the trial that is Fitzwilliam Darcy."

Darcy shook his head. "Am I truly as arrogant as you proposed the other night? I mean, I know that I have been since arriving in Hertfordshire because I did not want to be here, but am I always so?"

Bingley leaned back in his chair and folded his arms. "In a word, yes, though you have good reason to think highly of yourself. You have a large estate. Your income is significant. You have relations who are members of the peerage, and you were amongst the brightest of our lot at school."

"I will not deny that those things are true," Darcy said, "but the real question in the face of all that is: Is there ever truly a good reason to be as proud as I have been?"

Bingley shrugged. "I would like to say yes, but I know you will argue with me until I see your point and agree that there is not, which will likely be true since you think five miles ahead of me when you are pondering deeply, as you appear to be doing now."

"Returning to Miss Elizabeth," Hurst said. "I think you and she would suit quite well, and your estate and sister would be in good hands if they were in her care."

Bingley turned startled eyes to his brother-in-law. They had spoken about possibly broaching the subject of Darcy considering Miss Elizabeth as a wife, but Bingley had not thought to be quite so direct about it.

"Is that what you two were whispering about in the corner while I was attempting to read earlier?"

Hurst shrugged. "I would need more proof than speculation before I would be willing to state whether you are right or you are wrong."

Darcy chuckled.

Bingley blinked. That was not how he had expected his friend to respond.

"I was not reading. I was staring at words and flipping pages while considering what sort of accomplished lady I wish to have at my side for the rest of my life."

Bingley leaned forward, took up the bottle of port and placed the stopper firmly in the mouth of the bottle.

"What are you doing?" Hurst cried as he snatched the bottle from Bingley. "I will be having another glass, and neither you nor your sister can prevent it."

This time when Darcy chuckled, Bingley joined him.

"Did you not hear Darcy?" he asked Hurst. "He has been thinking about marrying. That is not a common topic about which he thinks."

"And you were worried that I have consumed one too many glasses of port and am speaking foolishly? Or were you concerned that if I had much more libation the thought of marrying would be washed away from my addled mind completely, never to return again?"

"Both, since I am not certain what to make of your admission. I truly thought we would have to work on you longer before you ever reached this point."

"You two truly are as bad as some housewives with all your tongue wagging and scheming! You do know that, do you not?"

Bingley shrugged while Hurst ignored the question completely in favour of filling his glass and then putting the bottle away from himself.

"Were you thinking about just a non-descript lady when you were contemplating earlier, or did you have one in particular in mind?" Hurst took a sip from his glass.

Darcy waggled his head from side to side. "If you will both promise not to be immediately offended if I stumble over my words, I will discuss this with you. I do not want to repeat the night of sleep I had last night."

"We will do our best, will we not, Bingley?"

"I will tell you if you have offended."

Darcy gave a single nod in acceptance. "I would appreciate it if you would." He shook his head. "If I have been so dreadful for so long, why have neither of you told me?"

Bingley smiled. "You are a rather imposing fellow."

"Because of my arrogance?"

Bingley shook his head. "No, because of your size. Neither of us is as tall or broad as you are."

Darcy rolled his eyes. "And I am given to violence, am I?"

"No, but I was not entirely certain you could not be provoked to it. Remember, we were with you after you returned from Ramsgate with your sister." And what a sight that had been. Bingley could not remember another time in all of his acquaintance with Darcy when the man had been so poorly groomed and quick to outbursts. His famous ability to hold himself in good regulation had been replaced by a man who seemed to carry a heavy, wounded and broken spirit.

"And we were certain that if there had been no law to prevent it, you would have allowed your cousin to dispatch the blackguard that harmed Miss Darcy if you did not take the pleasure of doing so into your own hands," Hurst said.

"I still do not think that excuses my friends from attempting to show me the error of my ways," Darcy protested with passion. "My mother would not be pleased to know what I have been."

"But," Bingley inserted before his friend could meander down a path towards despair, "she would be happy to see that you have not brushed off your error as if it were no more than a tiny bit of dust on an otherwise immaculate table, and I am positive that she would be pleased to see you attempting to mend your ways."

Darcy rose and paced to the door and back. He blew out a breath and shook his head. "But the real question – the one which has plagued me for some time – is: Would she or any of my family be pleased to know I am considering taking a lady of little standing and even less means as my wife?"

Bingley studied his friend. His eyes were filled with uncertainty, and his shoulders were slumped forward. It was very reminiscent of how he had looked for days after his sister's ordeal in Ramsgate.

"I have disappointed her once with my behaviour as it has been shown to me yesterday," he continued. "I would not wish to disappoint her again by making a poor choice for my wife."

Bingley opened his mouth to speak but before he could say a word, Hurst said, "Courtships often precede proposals. I do think you are getting the order of the cart and horse all turned about and backwards."

He drained the last of the port in his glass. "The Bennets are of little standing in London, but they are not in Hertfordshire. They would not be known in Derbyshire until they visited after you are married. The same could be said about town, I suppose. The connection is inferior when evaluated through the eyes of the same society that snubs you for having formed a friendship with Bingley, yet, your father was pleased with the connection."

"Because he and Bingley's father were friends," Darcy interrupted. "And that was different than this. Mr. Bennet is not a wealthy tradesman with connections."

"Is that the only reason our fathers were friends?" Bingley knew the answer but needed Darcy to say it.

"No, though it is how it began."

"And since Mr. Bennet has nothing to offer except his daughter and, I would venture to guess, a good discussion – you know how well-spoken the man is since you heard him when we were out hunting – you do not think that a friendship of any sort could develop there if your father were still alive?" Bingley pressed. This questioning and requestioning of things was not un-Darcy-like, but the inability to reason out the truth and claim it as such was. Apparently, Wickham had damaged more than Miss Darcy's heart; he had also shaken her brother's confidence far more than most would suspect. "Would your father discount Mr. Bennet out of hand?"

Darcy looked to the ceiling as he shook his head. "I do not know what he would think. I know what I would like for him to think, but I cannot say for certain that he would say that instead of telling me to look elsewhere."

"Perhaps," Hurst said, "we should start by considering how little you know about the Bennets. Mrs. Bennet was not altogether without sense today during her visit. I know she and her youngest daughters gave my wife and Caroline plenty of fodder to use to paint the connection in a negative light to both you and Bingley, but, would you truly be the first person of wealth and status to have a silly mother-in-law?"

Darcy sat down. "I suppose I would not be, but what about my uncle, the earl?"

"And what about your aunt, Lady Catherine?" Bingley countered. There was nothing terribly astute about Darcy's aunt.

"As the only married man among us, may I just say this: you are wise to consider the family to which you will be tied. If you have a wife with a trying sister, it could increase your outlay for good quality wine." He lifted his glass. "But eventually, she will marry."

"Or so we hope," Bingley muttered, eliciting a chuckle from his companions.

"However, even if she does not marry, and you are forced to house her for a time when Bingley's home needs a reprieve, she will not be the mother of your children, and it will not be her who will join you behind your chamber door and hold you close as you discuss all the trials and joys you share." He smiled. "I know Louisa is not much better than Caroline at times, but I love her, and she loves me. And that bond is worth the trial who is currently trying to capture your attention, Darcy, when she knows that your eyes are drawn to Miss Elizabeth, because she sees her connections and dowry as more acceptable than those of the Bennets. You do not want to be closing the door to your chamber and having to endure a wife who is acceptable but cannot engage your heart or mind as you need her to do."

"But there might be another who could do that and be acceptable."

"Perhaps," Hurst said with a shrug, "but I have never seen you so drawn to anyone like you are drawn to Miss Elizabeth. How much would you wager that you could find another who compares to her?"

Darcy heaved a great sigh.

"Pardon me, sir," a footman said as he entered the room. "Mrs. Nichols thought Mr. Bingley might like to know that Miss Bennet has improved enough to join the other ladies in the drawing room."

He most certainly did want to know that!

"Is the fire blazing?" he asked as he rose. "And does she need a blanket?"

"Mrs. Nichols said that Miss Elizabeth saw to it that Miss Bennet was well wrapped, and I did put an extra log on the fire, which she is sitting near."

"How long has she been there?"

"I do not know, sir, but I believe it has been a while, though likely not more than a quarter hour."

"Thank you for the information. We will join the ladies soon." He straightened his jacket and brushed the sleeves. Had he ever felt such an urgency as he did now to be at a lady's side and seeing to her care? He turned to his companions as the door closed behind the footman. "I am going to court Miss Bennet with the idea of marrying her if we truly suit as much as I think we do. I would not wager even two pence that I could ever find another like her, and you know I am far more easily persuaded to place a friendly bet than you are, Darcy."

He walked to the door of the dining room. "Will you join me?" he asked his dearest friend. "Not just in the drawing room but in pursuing what could be our greatest happiness?" His hand rested on the doorknob as he waited for Darcy to reply.

Darcy rose slowly and made himself presentable. Then, he picked up his glass of port, drained it of its contents, and nodded. "Whether Miss Elizabeth and I suit seems a study worth making, but I do not believe she likes me, and therefore, it might be an effort that is made in vain."

"It shall not be in vain if we have anything to do with it," Hurst said as he joined Bingley at the door.

Darcy shook his head and chuckled as he exited the door ahead of them. "Housewives. Both of you," he muttered.

Chapter 5

WHEN BINGLEY ENTERED THE drawing room where the ladies were gathered, he saw that his lovely Jane was just as the footman had described – well-wrapped and seated near a sizable fire. The sight made his heart glad. The smile she favoured him with when she saw him made his stomach do a little flip of delight. Yes, yes, yes, she was the one and only lady for him. He knew it to the depths of his being.

"Do not rise," he said to Miss Elizabeth, who looked ready to abandon her seat so that he could have it. "We can draw over two more chairs or perhaps my sisters would be so good as to provide some music for us and we can have their spots?"

Caroline's brow furrowed and her lips turned downward.

"What do you say, Darcy? Do you not think a bit of music would be just the thing?" His sister might not move for him, but she might for Darcy.

"I do," Hurst answered.

Darcy glanced around the group. "I am not opposed to music. I find it rather pleasant when Georgiana plays for me in the evenings when we are together."

"What would you like to hear?" Louisa asked as she pulled Caroline to her feet. "My sister would be happy to play for us, and when she tires, I can perhaps play something; though, I am not as proficient as she is."

"Why do we not ask Miss Elizabeth to play for us?" Caroline asked with a look of challenge for her brother.

"Because she is needed for her sister's care," Bingley replied. "If Miss Bennet needs something, I am certain she would be most comfortable if her sister were near to provide it."

Caroline's eyes flicked from him to Darcy, who was busily moving chairs. "But I am not certain I wish to play."

"Then, do not play," Darcy said as he placed a chair next to the one he had brought over for Bingley and sat down. "It matters not to me if you do or do not play."

"But you just said you find music in the evening pleasant," Louisa protested with a significant look at Caroline.

"I do find it pleasant, but that does not mean I require it."

Bingley smiled to himself. It seemed his friend was finally finding his footing and that both feet were firmly placed on the truth that Miss Elizabeth took precedence over placating either Louisa or Caroline.

"I am sure I could help Jane if needed." Caroline smiled coyly at Darcy.

"And I insist that it be Miss Elizabeth who provides aid if I cannot do it myself." Bingley made a small sweeping motion towards the piano. "Go play."

"I do not feel like it." Caroline pulled her hand free from Louisa's and sat back down. "We have seen so little of Miss Bennet, and you wish to rush us off so that you can have her attention all to yourself. I find that reprehensible. It is, after all, Louisa and I who are her particular friends, not you. And I quite imagine that Miss Elizabeth must grow weary of her constant care of her sister. Would it not be best to give her a reprieve?"

"I do not grow weary of caring for my sister," Miss Elizabeth protested. "I never would."

"Oh, come now, Miss Elizabeth, everyone grows tired of any activity at some point – it really does not matter how noble or mundane the task is. I am sure no one here would condemn you for wishing for a few moments to yourself." Her eyes cut towards Darcy. "Not even Mr. Darcy, and he is so very fond of his sister. Much like I am mine and you are yours."

"You seem to think that I value Mr. Darcy's opinion in the matter," Miss Elizabeth replied, "but I do not."

"Mr. Darcy's opinion does not hold value?" Louisa cried. "What an unusual, and dare I say, provincial opinion." She shook her head and clucked her tongue as if she were greatly concerned for Miss Elizabeth's well-being.

"I did not say that Mr. Darcy's opinion did not hold value. I said that in this matter, I do not value his opinion, meaning that I do not serve my sister or take my ease based upon whether Mr. Darcy thinks I should or should not. It is my heart that compels me. Nothing and no one else."

"Do you wish to play?" Jane asked her sister.

"You know I do not like to exhibit."

"Yes, but I do not want to keep you from what you wish to do."

Elizabeth took her sister's hands. "Dearest Jane, I believe you must still have a fever, for I can come up with no other reason for you to think I would make you fret over me."

Her tone was teasing. "You know as well as I do that I often do just what I want."

Jane laughed lightly and then coughed.

"Are you truly well enough to be out of bed?" Bingley did not want her to return to her room. He wanted her to stay and talk to him, but he also did not want to cause her to become worse once again.

"I am mending, and I shall not sit up too long. However, I must confess I was growing dreadfully tired of my room – not because it is not a lovely room, but because I have been in it for so long."

"I am happy to see that you felt well enough to join us," Darcy said. "We were quite concerned about you earlier today."

"Were you?" Miss Elizabeth pressed her fingers against her lips as if she had not meant to speak the question aloud.

"We were. Some of us more than others," he replied with a smile and a tip of his head towards Bingley. This brought a smile – whether willingly or unwillingly, Bingley could not tell – to Miss Elizabeth's lips.

"And that did not trouble you?"

"Perhaps at first, but then, I was made to see reason."

Miss Elizabeth's eyes grew wide.

"You were made to see reason about what?" Louisa asked.

Hurst chuckled.

"I do not see what is so humorous about my question," Louisa muttered.

"I have been made to see reason about my attitude toward Hertfordshire and its residents," Darcy explained before Hurst could tell his wife why he was chuckling. "I was not happy to leave my sister in town and come away to somewhere totally unfamiliar to me – especially since she had not been well – and I allowed it to colour my opinion, words, and actions. For that, I must apologize."

Miss Elizabeth's eyes were still wide and now her mouth hung the tiniest bit open.

"Do you now approve of the area and its inhabitants?" Louisa's tone was coloured with astonishment and a touch of disbelief.

Bingley relaxed into his chair. Louisa really was being very helpful – though she did not know it and would not be happy to find out how helpful she had been.

"I have not met all of the inhabitants," Darcy said, "and I am certain there are some of whom I would not approve. However, those who are with us this evening and those who visited us earlier are among those whom I would like to know better."

Ah, yes, Louisa did not like that reply.

"Indeed?" was all she said.

"I would not be opposed to visiting my friend in Hertfordshire regularly if he decides to remain at Netherfield."

Caroline sucked in a quick breath at Darcy's words.

"Charles's lease is only for a year," Louisa inserted.

"Leases can be renewed, and estates that were once for lease can be purchased," Hurst said. "If your brother likes the area and the house, I see nothing to keep him from staying for as long as he wishes."

Louisa turned horrified eyes to her husband. "I thought we agreed that Netherfield was not the estate for Charles."

Hurst shook his head. "No, that was you and Caroline. I said nothing."

"Precisely! You said nothing to oppose the idea. That is the same as agreeing."

Hurst stood and held his hand out to his wife. "I apologize, but it seems that my wife and I need to have a private conversation to clear up a misunderstanding." And with that, he led Louisa across the room and closer to the piano.

From where Bingley was sitting, he could see that Louisa was not pleased with anything that Hurst was saying. It was not the first time he had witnessed such a disagreement, and he expected that this one would eventually end the same way they all did – with Louisa reluctantly admitting that her husband might be right. She had a will of iron, but somehow, Hurst was able to bend it from time to time. That was one of the reasons why Bingley had been so willing to support the match. Hurst might look like a dandy who could be easily swayed from his position, but things were not always what they appeared to be.

He sifted his attention back to his immediate companions. Miss Elizabeth looked perplexed and was silent, Caroline seemed sullen and ill-at-ease, and Darcy? Well, he looked as if all was about to be right in his world. Of course, it would only be so if Miss Elizabeth could be persuaded to see him as Bingley knew Darcy to be.

"Has your sister told you that I have decided to host a ball?" Bingley asked Jane.

"Oh! Yes, she did. I think it is very kind of you to do so."

"It is not kind. It is self-serving. I rather enjoy dancing and the thought of spending a whole evening with you and my neighbours sounded like the most wonderfully self-indulgent thing when Miss Lydia presented the idea. I may even invite a few friends from town for Caroline's sake. We could do that, could we not? Netherfield has rooms enough for how many?"

"You are inviting more than the neighbours?" Caroline attempted to regulate her tone to one of simple surprise rather than one of disapproval but was unsuccessful.

"I am. There is not a single unattached gentleman in the area that I know of who would be a good match for you, so I thought it a fabulous idea to invite a few friends so you will have a whole cadre of dancing partners." He turned to Miss Elizabeth. "I had also noticed that there seemed to be fewer gentlemen than ladies at our last ball. I am not mistaken in that, am I?"

"No, no, you are not," she replied as her gaze flitted between Darcy and Caroline.

"They do not suit," he whispered in reply to her unspoken question. "Do you?" he asked Darcy.

"Oh," was all Miss Elizabeth said.

Darcy swallowed and then shook his head. "We do not."

Caroline expelled a breath as if she had been punched in the stomach. "I will see how many rooms can be made ready from Mrs. Nichols tomorrow." She rose. "If you will excuse me, I find I would like some music after all, as the company over here is not so pleasant as I had hoped for it to be." She gave Darcy a pointed look, though the expression was lost on him since he was not looking at her.

"That was very cruelly done," Miss Elizabeth whispered as Caroline moved away from them. "Perhaps I should go see if she needs someone to turn pages until her sister is available to assist."

"Your heart does you credit, Miss Elizabeth," Darcy said before she could move from her place.

"Does it indeed?" There was a touch of anger to her tone.

"I would not say it if I did not believe it to be true," Darcy replied.

"Mr. Darcy only answered a question honestly. Would you have had him lie instead?" Jane asked, causing her sister to turn her direction. "Do not blame Mr. Darcy for Mr. Bingley's actions."

Oh, dear, it seemed he had gone too far in his quest to see Darcy happily matched with Miss Elizabeth. He only hoped that in doing so he had not just ruined his own chances. He looked at Jane and then, her sister. "I am sorry. You are correct. I was cruel."

"I do not think it is us to whom you need to apologize." Jane's reprimand was gentle but firm.

"I am sorry to disagree with you," Bingley began, "but I do need to apologize to you and your sister for making you feel uncomfortable, and to my friend for forcing him to answer a question I knew he would not like to answer."

He sighed as the answer to the question Darcy had posed in the dining room became as clear as a star-filled sky on a cloudless night. "And you are right, Darcy, there is never a good reason for behaving poorly."

He shook his head and rose while continuing his explanation for what he had done. "I promise you that my intentions were not horrible. In fact, they were perhaps noble, for I was only thinking of my friend's happiness. I do hope that my stupidity has not utterly ruined my own chance of that." He sent a questioning look to Jane, who smiled and shrugged.

"Come, Miss Elizabeth. I will apologize to my sister, and you can offer your assistance if you still wish to do so."

She rose and joined him in crossing the room.

"Do not be surprised if Caroline is not welcoming to either of us. She knows Darcy likes you."

Elizabeth's steps faltered. "She knows what?"

"That Darcy likes you."

"No, he does not. He said I was…" Her words trailed off as if she had thought better of them.

"Yes, well, in that, he was lying."

Her head shook slowly as if she could not countenance what he was saying.

"I assure you that it is true." He motioned toward the piano, and then stepped close to his sister. "I have come to apologize, and Miss Elizabeth has come to offer her assistance in turning pages if it is required."

Caroline said nothing.

Bingley exhaled loudly. Why could his sister never make anything easy? "It was Miss Elizabeth who immediately wished to help you, and it was Miss Bennet who pointed out my error to me. You are fortunate to have two such caring friends."

He placed a hand on Caroline's shoulder. "I did not tell you anything you did not already know. However, I did it in such a way that it would dash your hopes and your heart – though, honestly, I did not think about your heart when I said what I did. I know that does not make what I did any better. In fact, it makes it all the worse. I should have considered your feelings even if you have not been careful to censor your words and have not considered how they may have caused hurt to Miss Elizabeth and Miss Bennet. Your lack of good manners does not justify mine."

Caroline glanced over her shoulder and for the first time, he saw the tears in her eyes. He groaned. She was always so cool and calculating. He had forgotten that she was even capable of crying. He handed her his handkerchief.

"I do hope you can forgive me."

She shrugged as her eyes moved to Miss Elizabeth. "Have you come to gloat?"

"No. I am not even sure what there is to gloat about."

Caroline huffed and rolled her eyes. "Surely you cannot be that stupid."

A portion of Bingley's remorse at causing his sister pain fled at the comment.

"Anyone can see that Mr. Darcy prefers you to me."

Miss Elizabeth shook her head. "Your brother has said something similar, but I assure you, I did not detect any admiration from Mr. Darcy, nor was I hoping to gain it."

Caroline's brows furrowed. "He watches you constantly."

"To find fault."

Caroline shook her head. "For all the reading you do, you are not as clever as some might suppose."

This caused Miss Elizabeth to fold her arms across her chest and glare at Caroline. "Do you need help with your pages or not?"

"Do you think you can manage it? I mean, someone who cannot even decipher when a gentleman admires her may not notice when one page needs moving and another should remain."

"He said I was tolerable and not handsome enough to tempt him before we even met. I do not see how that equates to the fact that I should then think he looks at me to admire me and not to disparage. I would say it is precisely the opposite, which is exactly how I have viewed any moment when I have noticed his attention turned my direction." She took her place at Caroline's side. "I will also have you know that I am very good at turning pages. I have four sisters for whom I have performed this very task."

Bingley simply stepped back and watched to see how things would conclude.

"Mr. Darcy said that to you? That you are not handsome or tempting?" Caroline's tone was filled with surprise and amusement.

"Not to me, but about me. I suggest you start playing."

Caroline laughed softly. "Well, he told me that you have fine eyes. Perhaps Mr. Darcy does not know what he thinks."

Well, there was some truth to that – or there had been.

"Then, perhaps you are not without hope," Miss Elizabeth said.

Oh, no, Caroline had no hope of snaring Darcy, and Bingley thought it best to not let such a thought even land for a second in his sister's mind. Therefore, leaning forward and poking his head in between Miss Elizabeth and his sister, he made certain they both knew where Darcy stood on the matter.

"I assure you," he said, "that Darcy has determined what he thinks, and he will not be joining my family unless I can be so fortunate as to persuade Miss Bennet to accept me and add me to hers." He winked at Miss Elizabeth as he said it and then placed a kiss on Caroline's cheek before quickly taking himself back to his no-longer-confused friend and the lady he hoped to convince to marry him.

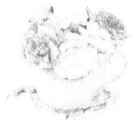

Chapter 6

TWO DAYS LATER, BINGLEY stood just outside Netherfield's library, listening. He smiled as Darcy concluded his
tale about being locked in the wine cellar for two hours
with his cousin when he was a child.

Darcy had said that he intended to read for some time
when Bingley had inquired about his plans before leaving
the room. However, it had not taken much more than
five minutes before Darcy's book had been abandoned to
his lap, and he had asked Miss Elizabeth about what she
was reading. This had then led to a discussion of favourite
pursuits which had, in turn, wound its way to the story
Darcy had just shared.

As Bingley peered at them through the small opening
created by his not closing the door completely when he
had left, he had to admit that they both seemed quite
content in each other's presence. Both sat in a relaxed
posture and wore happy expressions. He had yet to hear a
sharp retort from Miss Elizabeth, and Darcy had yet to say
anything requiring such a response. Another day or two
of several hours spent together should surely strengthen
the relationship between them into what Bingley hoped

would be a fine, stout love – or the budding of such, at the very least.

He knew that once Darcy proved to himself that a friendship was worthy of his time, the man's loyalty would immediately begin to build great stone walls surrounding him and his friend. Bingley also knew, and was thankful for, just how difficult it was to shift that loyalty once it was formed. It took more than just a little stumble or trifling misunderstanding to break through it.

However, once a fissure in the fortifications of the friendship occurred, the likelihood of those ties ever being rebuilt, rather than crushed to rubble and removed, was unlikely. And understanding all that about his dearest friend, he recognized that what he was now witnessing was the formation of an imperviable fortification.

"He is quite determined to win her, is he not?" Hurst's whisper made Bingley jump and clutch his heart, for he was not certain it would remain where it was supposed to be but would rather leap right out of his chest and scamper away in fright.

His brother-in-law chuckled. "You should never be so engrossed in eavesdropping that you forget your surroundings."

"Yes, well, we all make mistakes."

"Speaking of that, Louisa has convinced Caroline that the best way to extract revenge upon you and Darcy for the slight she was made to bear the other night is by marrying better than either of you do." He smiled smugly.

Bingley eyed his sister's husband suspiciously. "Did Louisa come up with that idea or was it you?"

"Louisa." He paused and looked up and down the corridor. "She came to the conclusion just after I made a not-so-flippant comment about something similar."

"I never took you to be someone so conniving," Bingley said with a shake of his head. Hurst often appeared rather nonchalant and often not aware of what was transpiring around him. If one did not spend any amount of time with him beyond a soiree here and there, one would think him a bit lacking in intelligence.

Bingley had fallen into that error before Hurst had married Louisa, but he was slowly learning that he had been too hasty in forming an opinion about the man. They were, quite to Bingley's surprise, becoming quite good friends. He had truly never imagined that either of his sisters would marry fellows who would be more than tolerable acquaintances.

"However," he continued, "that does make you an even better match for my sister, and a good ally for me, so I am happy for it."

The two of them shared a chuckle – quietly. The door to the library was open a crack after all, and neither of them wanted their observations of the couple within to be discovered.

"Do you remember the friend of mine who called on Caroline several times last season?" Hurst asked as Darcy once again looked up from his book and said something to Miss Elizabeth that made her smile. "What did he say?"

Bingley gave him an exasperated look. "How can I hear both him and you?" He nodded down the hall, and the two of them tip-toed away from the door. "Now, tell me why I am thinking about your friend. Warren, was it not? And did he not have a title in his future?"

"He has both a title and a fortune in his very near future. As I hear it, his grandfather is not doing well. They have taken him to Bath to see if the waters can help, but it is a fool's errand – that is in the words of my friend." Hurst shrugged when Bingley's eyes grew wide at how casually Hurst was speaking about the final demise of a friend's relation. "They are not overly close. His father has not visited his grandfather in twenty years at least. He was a hard man, who wrote his son out of the will in favour of his grandson, and, according to Warren's father, 'the old mule' does not deserve an easy end. That, however, is neither here nor there as the story applies to us being well-rid of a sister."

"Continue."

"I sent him an express before breakfast the day after you angered Caroline and my wife by putting Darcy's suit of Miss Elizabeth forward." He pulled an envelope from his pocket. "And I have just received his reply. He is delighted to hear about Darcy's possible courtship and would be delighted to receive and accept an invitation to your ball. He has asked that he be allowed to arrive a day early so that you and he can discuss the particulars of his intentions regarding Caroline."

"He cannot possibly still wish to marry her! Did she not send him away twice last season?" The man had seemed extremely persistent about presenting his suit to Caroline despite her less than charming rebuffs of him. "Do we trust that he is not playing some scheme? She has her own fortune, you know."

"I am well aware of Caroline's financial position. It has been brought up in exasperation several times within my hearing as Louisa and Caroline have been lamenting

Darcy's lack of proper sense in preferring a pair of fine eyes to a tidy sum of money." The look on Hurst's face when he said this let Bingley know precisely how little his brother-in-law had enjoyed having to listen to those conversations.

"Allow me to apologize again. I know it was not well done, but Caroline had to be put off and Miss Elizabeth had to be put forward." He was still nearly positive that he had acted correctly even if he had done so in an awkward fashion. The companionship that Darcy and Miss Elizabeth seemed to be sharing at this moment in the library was proof of that, was it not?

Hurst sighed. "I know, and I am not upset with you. I am just tired of hearing about Caroline's chances to marry well, which brings me back to Warren. He is not playing. He and Darcy are rather similar in that way, for there is not even the slightest bend in his character. He is as straight an arrow as there ever was. Added to that, he has a fortune that is to come to him which he will add to the tidy sum that is already his. He assures me that the estate he will claim once his grandfather passes is exceptional and does not want from updating since his grandfather always had to have the best. Warren is everything, to the tiniest detail, that Louisa is promoting to Caroline, and I intend to bring his name up in conversation with Louisa later today if you will allow me to do so."

The fellow did sound promising, but there was still the matter of his sister's happiness. She would have never been completely happy with Darcy. She thought she would have been, but Bingley knew better. They simply did not suit. As much as she annoyed him, he did not want to see her miserable. "Do you think Caroline will be happy with him?"

"I do not know. I believe it is possible, but only she can tell us that, which is why I think we should allow the man to pursue where he can and to the end he wishes with the stipulation that the power of final acceptance or refusal is where it should be – with Caroline."

That made sense. "It will make her slightly unbearable to be around if she chooses him, will it not? For she will have something to hold over me and Darcy – and Miss Elizabeth."

"Aye, but she will also be married and at her estate in Suffolk for most of the year. I am sure that I will be in her company more often than you – thanks to the closeness she shares with my wife. It would be nice to have my friend there to make the arrangement a pleasure rather than just something to be endured."

The thought of Hurst being blessed by having a good friend so closely related – much like Bingley and Darcy would be if things continued to go well – made the decision easy. "Then, I say we arrange a meeting with the man and make sure he is on our list of guests for the ball."

Hurst rubbed his hands together. "I say! We should charge for our services. We are quite the matchmaking duo."

Bingley chuckled. "We have not succeeded in seeing a match completed yet."

"I will thank you not to speak for me on that account," Hurst replied as they once again moved toward the library door. "I am happily married, so that makes one match for me."

"Does that count?"

"According to my rules, yes."

The door to the library opened just as they reached it.

"Are you done reading already?" Bingley asked Darcy in surprise.

"I am never done reading," his friend teased. "However, it is a sunny day, and Miss Elizabeth agreed that we should not spend all of it indoors. Therefore, we are going to the garden for a walk. Do you wish to join us?"

"I would welcome some fresh air, but I would not wish to make a nuisance of myself," Bingley replied. However, it would be easier to observe and hear what was transpiring in the garden if he were there rather than peeking out a window.

"I was going to see if Jane wished to join me," Miss Elizabeth said. "She was feeling quite well this morning and only went upstairs to rest at my request."

A walk with Miss Bennet? Well, now, that would be a lovely thing. "If you are certain that it will not do her any harm, I would be delighted to offer her my arm for her support."

Miss Elizabeth smiled. "I am certain that such a thing will only aid in her recovery, which I do believe is nearly complete. In fact, we were talking, just this morning, about returning home on the morrow."

"So soon?" That was not what was needed. Darcy needed at least one more day with Miss Elizabeth, and Bingley wished for all the rest of his own with Miss Bennet.

"We have trespassed on your kindness long enough. There is no danger in my sister being moved, especially if she can attempt a short walk in the sunshine."

"Then, perhaps it is best if she does not attempt it."

Miss Elizabeth's eyes widened at the comment.

"I have not had very many opportunities to be in company with her, and I would like a few more," Bingley explained.

This brought back Miss Elizabeth's smile.

"It might be best," Darcy inserted, "if Miss Bennet attempts the walk today, and then takes the day tomorrow to evaluate how little or greatly the exercise affected her. Monday would be soon enough to return to Longbourn, do you not think?"

"You both seem very determined to keep us here," she replied with a light laugh.

"We are," Darcy said. "I find your company to be quite refreshing. Bingley is a consummate host and rarely allows me time to be bored. However, he has yet to have a discussion about literature with me that was not done in preparation for some class at school."

"Do you not read?" Miss Elizabeth asked Bingley.

"I read. I just do not enjoy it as much as my friend, nor do I find it entertaining to decipher the deeper meanings. I would rather leave a piece of prose or poetry to do what it was intended to do – provide a diversion for me."

"Does that not relegate the writing to being something trivial and of no great importance?"

Bingley chuckled. Yes, Miss Elizabeth was the perfect match for Darcy.

"No," he answered, "it only deprives me of the drudgery of making it of greater importance than I find it to be. I do not deem work created simply to be a pleasant diversion to be of lesser value than that which is constructed to make my friend think great thoughts and drone on and on about them." He held up a finger as a thought struck him. "Indeed, I think that perhaps the only true purpose is diversion – for me the diversion comes in the reading and for my friend, it comes in the picking apart and putting back together." Yes, yes, that had to be it. He did have his moments of brilliance.

"You seem very certain of your opinion, sir."

"I assure you I am. However, I am also just as certain that my thoughts shall be thoroughly studied, and I will be informed of their errors in due course if there, indeed, be any errors." He clapped his friend on the shoulder. "And now I have provided even more entertainment for my friend and possibly you?"

Elizabeth laughed. "You most certainly have. You have presented a worthy topic upon which to ponder."

"We can discuss it in the garden if you would like?" Darcy offered.

"At this moment, I would like nothing better. Allow me to go get my wrap and my sister, and then we can debate the proposition Mr. Bingley has provided."

"May I escort you to your sister?"

Miss Elizabeth declared that to be an excellent thing, and soon, she and Darcy were halfway up the grand staircase.

"I do not want to take a walk in the garden," Hurst said, causing Bingley to jump once again.

How had he forgotten his brother-in-law was still standing with him? He put a hand to his forehead. No, he did not feel ill.

Hurst chuckled. "You would make a dreadful spy."

"Undoubtedly, I would, but it seems I have done an excellent job of selecting the perfect lady for Darcy."

"So it would appear. Can you imagine Caroline trying to participate in a discourse about the intent of writing?"

Hurst asked as the two of them stood watching the pair on the stairs.

Bingley laughed. "I dare say you would find her engaged in such a thing before you would ever find me doing it – unless, of course, Miss Bennet is the sort to enjoy such discussions." He hoped she did not. She had not seemed the sort who would, but if she was... "I think I could tolerate it if I was listening to her state her reasons. I do find her more enjoyable to listen to than Darcy."

Hurst sighed. "We are capable of enduring many conversations we would not normally pursue when it comes to the ladies we love." And with that, he continued on his way toward the drawing room where Louisa and Caroline were planning a ball.

Perhaps by the time that soiree was ended, with a bit of good fortune falling on them, there would not be an unattached gentleman or lady left of those who currently resided at Netherfield.

Chapter 7

"YOU WERE RIGHT," DARCY said as he joined Bingley at the bottom of the steps to wait for their ladies to join them.

Two days earlier, they had stood at this very spot doing the same exact thing, but today, they were not waiting to go for a walk. No, today, they were preparing to escort their ladies home. Jane was so much improved that one would almost believe she had never been ill. Bingley was happy to see that, of course, but also disheartened by it as it meant that there was no longer any reason for her to remain at Netherfield.

"Are you not going to ask me about what you were correct?" Darcy asked when Bingley did not reply to his first comment.

"I must apologize. I was lost in my thoughts about how a return to health is in this circumstance is bittersweet; however, now that you have my full attention, you may praise my genius as it deserves."

Darcy chuckled. "I will not go so far as to call it genius, though I will admit it is perhaps the most astute you have ever been." He straightened his jacket as he spoke and then checked his watch. "Miss Elizabeth is precisely the best sort of accomplished lady. I grant that I have not witnessed all the particulars of her accomplishments, for we have not called on any tenants nor have we had the opportunity to go over an account book or arrange furniture and pick paint. But, be that as it may, I have observed and been quite delighted with her keen mind and caring heart. She has forgiven me readily for my atrocious behaviour, she fairly dotes on Miss Bennet, and our discussions about many things have been lively and proven that on many items of great importance, we are agreed. For all those reasons, I intend to speak to her father to make my position as a hopeful match for his daughter known."

He looked behind them and then up the stairs. Darcy was rarely good at remaining still when he was eager to begin a task.

"You should also know that I am determined to be successful, and I will do whatever you might need me to do to ensure your success with Miss Bennet. She is as you proclaimed her last night, quite lovely and perfectly designed to be Mrs. Bingley. Added to that, my happiness would not be complete without yours being just as happy."

Ah, there was the Darcy that Bingley had grown to love as dearly as a brother. This was the man who had been missing for some months now – ever since that fateful trip to Ramsgate.

"Does this mean then that you understand why I had to conspire with Hurst regarding you and Miss Elizabeth?"

Darcy nodded. "I think I do."

Above them, the ladies who held their future happiness in their hands were just beginning their descent of the stairs.

"Are you certain you feel well enough to endure the carriage ride to your home?" Bingley asked Jane, who smiled sweetly while her eyes flickered with amusement.

"I am quite sure that no ill will befall me from the excursion."

"But perhaps we should just take one more walk around the garden to ensure that you are well, and tomorrow you can return home."

"And tomorrow, you will say the same thing, just as you have for the past two days."

He extended his hand to her when she came close enough for him to do so.

"If it helps you bear our parting, I shall miss being here," she added. "You have been a most gracious host. I dare say that I have never rested quite so well while sick as I did here."

"That," Miss Elizabeth inserted, "is because Mama was not here to worry over you at every cough."

Bingley loved the sound of Jane's sweet laugh. It was soft and gentle, but then, she seemed incapable of being anything other than soft and gentle.

"Is it only the house and tranquility which you will miss?" Bingley asked hopefully.

"No."

She gave him only that word in reply, but it was enough. He glanced at his friend and Miss Elizabeth.

"It would be quite the thing if we could always be in company such as we are now."

Jane's cheeks grew rosy. "I would like that very much."

"Are you about to abscond with our dear Jane without allowing her to say her farewell to us?" Louisa stood at the door to the drawing room that was just beyond the table with the small urn on it to Bingley's right.

"Perhaps not just as we are now," Bingley said before turning to his sister. "I would do so, but I am quite certain that both Miss Bennet and Miss Elizabeth are much better at doing things properly than I am."

"Charles," Louisa scolded. "You have been taught impeccable manners. Perhaps it is the company you keep which has ruined them."

"Did you hear that, Darcy? My sister thinks your manners are lacking."

"I said no such thing! It is country society which has caused you to forget yourself."

"Darcy's is the company which I keep most regularly no matter where I am – unless, of course, he is not with me." He and Jane walked down the corridor ahead of Darcy and Miss Elizabeth.

"Did you hear?" Louisa asked as they reached the door where she stood. "We have just received our first acceptance of an invitation to our ball."

"Have we sent out invitations?" Bingley knew they had not.

"None have been formally sent, of course," Louisa answered with an air of importance as she led them all into the room. "But Hurst mentioned it in a letter to his dear friend Mr. Warren, and we received an express not two hours ago informing Hurst that his friend is keen to join us." She smoothed her skirts after sitting. "We have some reason to believe that it is not just my husband whom he is eager to see." She cut a sly look at Caroline. "He is a gentleman of some standing."

"Is he, indeed?" Jane asked.

"Oh, very. I dare say he shall be a little higher than even Mr. Darcy soon." Here she sighed before leaning forward and whispering. "His grandfather is not well, you see, and Mr. Warren is his heir."

"His grandfather is a baronet," Caroline added.

"Which means Mr. Warren will have a title," Louisa said.

"And," Caroline continued, "he shared a little about his estate when he called on me last season. It sounds quite lovely and is not at all small."

"He sounds promising. Is he handsome?" Jane asked.

"He is quite fashionable," Louisa answered. "All of Hurst's friends are."

"Is fashionable the same as handsome?" Miss Elizabeth asked.

Louisa chuckled softly. "Forgive me. I forgot that you are not acquainted with how things are spoken of in fine society. Yes, Mr. Warren is handsome and always impeccably dressed. He knows what to do as well as when and how to do it. I have never heard him utter a word that was not just what it should be."

"That is because you have not been in a room where it is just us men," Hurst inserted. "Warren is not perfect, my dear."

"As I said, he knows *when* to do things as they should be done."

"And is he interesting?" Miss Elizabeth asked.

"Oh, very. He has a box at the theatre and never wants for the best invitations. And to be seated next to him at dinner is pure pleasure, for one is always assured of a good conversation."

"Then, I dare say, Mr. Hurst, that you are wrong." Miss Elizabeth's words were accompanied by a teasing smile. "It truly sounds as if Mr. Warren is perfection in human form. However, I suppose we shall get to judge that for ourselves when we meet him."

"Yes, I am anxious to make his acquaintance," Jane agreed. "It is always nice to meet new friends, is it not?"

"I say there is nothing better," Bingley answered, "but Darcy would be hesitant to lend his agreement."

"I have met many people whom I would rather not have met," Darcy admitted.

"But does that count?" Miss Elizabeth asked. "Were those people friends or just people with whom you once spent a few minutes?"

"One of them is his aunt," Bingley whispered and then made a show of shuddering.

"Aunts are relations. We have no choice but to meet them. The choice in those cases lies with whether or not we choose to claim them as friends."

At that reply, Bingley once again congratulated himself on selecting such a fine match for his friend. Not only did she possess the sort of quick wit that loved nothing better than to debate the nuances of a matter, but her spirit was bright and lively enough to complement his friend's more solemn outlook.

"Pardon me, sir," Mrs. Nichols the housekeeper said, "but you wished to know when your carriage was ready, and it is."

"Have the Miss Bennets' things been secured?"

"Yes, sir. Everything is as it should be."

Bingley had to disagree with that, for if things were as he thought they should be, Jane and her sister would not be leaving Netherfield and Caroline would already be Lady Warren.

As it stood, however, those things would not be until after the new year had begun. Bingley's ball would be a success and secure his position in the Hertfordshire area as a host whose invitations were eagerly sought. Darcy would acquit himself well on calls and at soirees. Ridiculous relations and troublesome former friends would be endured, and through it all, the love that had blossomed during Jane's illness and because of Bingley's interference between Darcy and Miss Elizabeth would grow until one day in May, after licenses had been acquired, registers had been signed, and the servants were beginning the task of putting Netherfield back in order after a wedding breakfast, Bingley once again found himself standing at the bottom of the grand staircase.

Yes, Bingley thought to himself, this was perfection. Jane would no longer leave his home. And when Darcy finally left, it would not be alone, for Elizabeth would go with him. That was a sad thought.

"I do not think I will keep Netherfield," he announced.

"Do you not?' Jane asked in surprise. "Where will we go if we are not here?"

"To Derbyshire. What do you think of the idea? I think it would be quite fabulous for us all to be able to gather under one roof nearly whenever we wanted, and for our children to be friends."

His question was met with one of Jane's best sorts of smiles – the one that curled her lips in happiness and made delight dance in her eyes. And Bingley knew before she spoke that his idea was to her liking.

"I think it is a fabulous idea."

"Then, you will not be disappointed that you will not be mistress of Netherfield as you expected to be when we joined our hands before the parson this morning?" He likely should have presented this as a possibility before that, but he had not completely decided if he should even truly consider it until just now.

"I did not marry you because of where you live, Mr. Bingley," she said as sternly as she was able to do while still smiling.

"Then, Mrs. Bingley, why did you marry me? I have heard from both my sisters that knowing a gentleman's fortune and the state of his estate are of utmost importance when pledging to love him forever."

Jane, as well as Darcy and Elizabeth, laughed at the comment.

"Why, Mr. Bingley, I have married you for love, of course. Have I not declared it enough?"

He lifted her hand to his lips. "That is something I shall never tire of hearing. I do love you, my dearest Jane." He sighed. "Shall we take a walk in the garden?" He glanced around the group. "I am not sure when we will next all have the chance to do so." The Darcys would leave for Pemberley tomorrow.

"I think that is an excellent idea," Darcy answered. "What say you, Elizabeth?"

"I rarely refuse a walk," she answered with a laugh. "Especially when it is with you."

When Darcy gathered Elizabeth into his arms and kissed her soundly, Bingley could not have stopped himself from grinning if he had wanted to.

The change in his friend over the past few months had been remarkable. He walked with less of an air of importance. He smiled even when he was alone – or thought he was. He paused when in the middle of a task for no apparent reason at all. It was as if the ever-moving, constantly searching, rigidly proper master of Pemberley had finally found that for which he had been seeking – a lady whose greatest accomplishment did not lie in how many books she had read or if there was a certain something in the way she spoke or an air in her walk. It rested within her, in a heart that quite willingly gave him a home.

"I have done very well, have I not?" Bingley whispered to Jane.

Darcy made no move to break his kiss.

"I have quite convinced him that your sister is the best sort of accomplished lady, have I not?" he said a little louder.

Darcy still did not stop kissing Elizabeth.

"Well, then, we shall be in the garden when you are through," he said rather loudly.

Jane giggled as she let him lead her down the hall toward the door.

"You know, my dear, at one time, Darcy thought that you were not good enough for me." This was not news to Jane. Bingley – and Darcy because of Bingley – had discussed that topic with both Jane and Elizabeth, as well as their father, but never their mother.

"Bingley!" The word rumbled down the hall after him. "I have already made my apologies for that and am beginning to think it is the other way around."

"Me? Not good enough for my wife? I think you may finally have the right of that." He placed his hat on head and stepped out into a bright spring afternoon that reflected

perfectly the joy he both held in his heart and looked forward to in his future.

If you enjoyed this book, be sure to let others know by leaving a review.
~*~*~
Want to know when other Leenie books will be available?
You can always know what's new with my books by subscribing to my mailing list.

leeniebrown.com/subscribe

More Books by Leenie

You can find all of Leenie's books at this link

bit.ly/LeenieBBooks
where you can explore the collections below.
~*~

Dash of Darcy and Companions Collection

Marrying Elizabeth Series

Sweet Possibilities and Sweet Extras

Willow Hall Romances

The Choices Series

Darcy Family Holidays

Darcy and... An Austen-Inspired Collection

Teatime Tales (Sweet Austen-inspired Novelettes)

Other Pens

Touches of Austen

Nature's Fury and Delights (Sweet Regency Novelettes)

About Leenie

Leenie Brown has always been a girl with an active imagination, which, while growing up, was both an asset, providing many hours of fun as she played out stories, and a liability, when her older sister and aunt would tell her frightening tales. At one time, they had her convinced Dracula lived in the trunk at the end of the bed she slept in when visiting her grandparents!

Although it has been years since she cowered in her bed in her grandparents' basement, she still has an imagination which occasionally runs away with her, and she feeds it now as she did then — by reading!

Her heroes, when growing up, were authors, and the worlds they painted with words were (and still are) her favourite playgrounds! Now, as an adult, she spends much of her time in the Regency world, playing with the characters from her favourite Jane Austen novels and those of her own creation.

When she is not traipsing down a trail in an attempt to keep up with her imagination, Leenie resides in the beautiful province of Nova Scotia with her two sons and her very own Mr. Brown (a wonderful mix of all the best of Darcy, Bingley, and Edmund with a healthy dose of the teasing Mr. Tilney and just a dash of the scolding Mr. Knightley).

Connect with Leenie

Subscribe to Leenie's Mailing List:

leeniebrown.com/subscribe
Website: *leeniebrown.com*
Patreon: patreon.com/LeenieBrown
Facebook: facebook.com/LeenieBrownAuthor
MeWe: mewe.com/p/leeniebrown1
Instagram: @leeniebbooks
E-mail: *LeenieBrownAuthor@gmail.com*